1 pt.

# Beady Bear

**Also by Don Freeman**

MOP TOP

FLY HIGH, FLY LOW

THE NIGHT THE LIGHTS WENT OUT

NORMAN THE DOORMAN

SPACE WITCH

CYRANO THE CROW

COME AGAIN PELICAN

SKI PUP

THE TURTLE AND THE DOVE

**By Lydia and Don Freeman**

PET OF THE MET

CHUGGY AND THE BLUE CABOOSE

# BEADY BEAR

## STORY AND PICTURES BY DON FREEMAN

THE VIKING PRESS  •  NEW YORK

For
Marjorie Rankin
of the Children's Room
of the Santa Barbara Public Library

**Eighth printing November 1966**

Copyright 1954 by Don Freeman
First published by The Viking Press in September 1954
Published on the same day in the Dominion of Canada
by the Macmillan Company of Canada Limited

**Pic Bk**

Lithographed in the U. S. A. by Reehl Litho Co.

Beady was a fuzzy toy bear who belonged to a boy named Thayer.

Hide-and-seek was their favorite fun.

From time to time Beady would suddenly stop and topple over—
kerplop! He'd come unwound!

Then Thayer would always go find him and take his key
and gently wind him.

8

Once Beady was all wound up, he wanted to keep on playing.

And yet when Thayer went to bed Beady knew he ought to, too.

One winter's day Thayer went away. Just when he'd be back
he didn't say.

Being all alone for the first time, Beady amused himself by
looking at a book.

12

"Why hasn't anybody told me this before?" said Beady sadly to himself.

"I wonder if there could be a cave for me away up in those hills?"

Taking a long look through Thayer's shiny telescope he searched
the side of the hill until — he spied

15

a cave!

So he left a note.

Up the hill he climbed and climbed.

At last!

He could hardly believe his beady eyes — it was just his size!

"A perfect place for a brave bear like me!" sighed Beady.

"And yet it's awfully dark and stilly here inside! And a wee bit chilly, really!"

That night Beady couldn't sleep a wink. "It's because of these sharp stones, I think.

"There's something I need in here to make me truly happy.
I wonder what it could be?"

"Oh, I know!" and up he got and out he trotted down the snowy
hillside to his house far below.

And what should he bring back but his very own little pillow!

"This is more like it!" said Beady as he bedded down for the
rest of the night.

"But there still seems to be something missing!"

So down the hill he trotted again

and brought back—of all things—a flashlight. But as soon as he
settled down he knew

there was something more a bear needed to be truly happy.
"What good is a light without something to read?" said Beady.

The evening papers, indeed!

Now what more could a bear ask for?

Well, after reading all the papers, Beady began to worry and wonder. "Maybe it's some toys I need..."

35

At this very moment he heard a loud noise outside.
"It's a bear!" said Beady.

"I must be brave! This is probably his cave!"

The noise grew louder and louder as Beady moved along, ever
so slowly and shakily. Suddenly he came to a stop —

and over he toppled — kerplop! "Who's there?" cried Beady,
upside down.

"It's me, Thayer! I'm looking for my bear!"

But from inside the cave now came not a sound — Beady was
much too embarrassed, lying there on the ground!

"Well, hello, Beady boy! I thought I'd find you in this place.
That's why I brought along your key, just in case!

"For goodness' sakes, Beady, don't you know you need a key?

"And me?"

"Yes, but if I need you, who do you need?"

"I need Beady!"

So down the hill to home they went, paw in hand and hand in paw,

and when Beady went to bed that night, he was the truly
happiest bear you ever saw.